Thayer Memorial Library

P.O. Box 5 ✧ 717 Main Street ✧ Lancaster, Massachusetts 01523 ✧ (978)368-8928 ✧ Fax (978)368-8929

Pete Makes a Mistake

Emily Arnold McCully

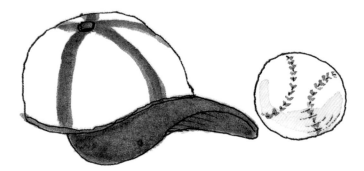

I Like to Read®

Holiday House / New York

Library of Congress Cataloging-in-Publication Data
McCully, Emily Arnold, author, illustrator.
Pete makes a mistake / Emily Arnold McCully. — First edition.
pages cm. — (I like to read)
Summary: Distracted by his friends, Pete the pig forgets
to give Gert an invitation to Rose's party.
ISBN 978-0-8234-3387-2 (hardcover)
[1. Parties—Fiction. 2. Behavior—Fiction. 3. Pigs—Fiction.] I. Title.
PZ7.M478415Pd 2015
[E]—dc23
2014032160

ISBN 978-0-8234-3422-0 (paperback)

Come to my party!
Sunday 3:00
Rose Pig

"Can you take these
to my friends?" says Rose.
"What will you give me?"
says Pete.
"Cake," says Rose.

Pete goes.

He takes a
note to Nell.

And he takes
a note to Don.

Pete sees his friends.

He puts Gert's note
in his pocket.

Rose gets
balloons.

She makes
a cake.

She hangs stars.

She gets some rest.

On Sunday she waits.

Don and Nell come.

They have juice.
"Where is Gert?"
Rose asks.

"Why didn't she come?"

"Let's look for her,"
say Don and Nell.

Gert wants to play with her friends.

But Nell is not home.

And Don is not home.

Gert looks for Rose.

"Rose had a party,"
she says.
"And she didn't ask
me to come."

Rose, Don and Nell
go to Gert's house.

"Where is Gert?"
they ask her dad.
"I don't know," he says.
"She went out."

They wait for Gert
to come back.

Then Pete looks
in his pocket.
He sees the note
for Gert.
"Oh no!" he says.

He runs to Gert's house.

Rose, Nell and Don
are there.
"Here is Gert's note," he says.
"I am sorry."

"We must find Gert!"
says Rose.
"I want some juice,"
says Don.

They go back to Rose's house
for juice. Gert is there!
"Here is your note," says Rose.

"Now we can have a party."

And they all have cake.
Even Pete.

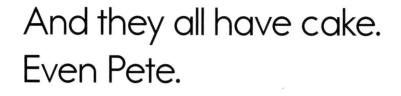